For Alfie, who arrived one starry night, with love, Dad x

First U.S. edition 2009

Library of Congress Cataloging-in-Publication Data is available.
Library of Congress Catalog Card Number 2008935208
ISBN 978-0-7636-4425-3

2 4 6 8 10 9 7 5 3 1

Printed in China

This book was typeset in Bokka Solid.
The illustrations were done in acrylic on paper.

Edited by A.J. Wood
Designed by Mike Jolley

A TEMPLAR BOOK

An imprint of
Candlewick Press
99 Dover Street
Somerville, Massachusetts 02144
www.candlewick.com

Bob's Best ever Friend

Simon Bartram

templar books
an imprint of Candlewick Press

It was a Tuesday morning in space,
and nothing much was happening.

Since there were no space tourists visiting the
Moon that day, Bob, the **Man on the Moon**,
had finished all of his Moon work by ten o'clock.

Bob's friends Billy and Sam were away on a trip to
Pluto, visiting a most exciting pet show.
They hoped to see some alien animals there,
but Bob thought they'd be disappointed. After all,
everyone knows there's no such thing as aliens,
especially not alien **animals**.

With nobody to talk to, Bob felt a little glum, so
he decided to go for a bounce on his bouncy castle.
But bouncing without a friend just wasn't as fun.

Quite frankly, Bob was a bit **lonely**.

To cheer himself up, Bob went for a quick spin around the universe in his rocket.

Nothing much was happening there either.

Unfortunately, most of the planets were closed for the winter. So Bob stopped off on a passing asteroid to enjoy a nice cup of tea and a corned beef sandwich for lunch. The view was beautiful. It was just a shame that he had **no one** to share it with.

"What I need," Bob said to himself, "is a **best-ever** friend, a chum—someone to help with intergalactic missions and jigsaw puzzles— a pal who'll always be by my side."

But **where** on earth could he find a friend like that?

For the rest of the day, Bob pondered his problem, until it was time to return to Earth for a nice supper of fish sticks and peas. As a Tuesday treat, he allowed himself to eat in front of the TV.

The newscaster was warning that a troublesome asteroid had been causing havoc elsewhere in the solar system and was now in danger of crashing into Earth. Bob was **glued** to the screen.

He wished he had someone to watch the program with—it was **SO** exciting.

As he sipped his cocoa in bed, Bob decided that he would start looking for a best-ever friend tomorrow morning.

Bob pedaled as fast as he could to the rocket launch pad and in a super-fast **flash**, changed into his man-on-the-moon suit.

He needed to reach the moon before the first "moon tours" tourist spaceship arrived—there were snacks and entertainments to prepare.

After he clambered aboard and flicked lots of switches, his rocket began to rumble and Bob counted down. . . .

5 . . . 4 . . . 3 . . . 2 . . . 1 . . . **LIFTOFF!!**

By quarter to six, he was **zooming** toward the golden moon, and by six o'clock, he was there.

The best tea in town was served at the MOON-SOUP PIT-STOP CAFÉ. Bob felt quite at home among the Moon pictures and decorations, although sometimes he did call it the MOON-STOP PIT-SOUP CAFÉ by mistake.

Bob wondered if anyone would recognize the world-famous Man on the Moon and sit with him, but no one did. So Bob sat quietly and nibbled his favorite "Moon-Soup Crater Cake" by himself. He knew it was really just a doughnut, but it was tip-top tasty all the same. It was a shame there was no time for seconds, but night was falling and Bob had a job to do. . . .

The Moon was waiting!

$9.99
MOON TOURS with BOB
DEPART 5:50 pm SHARP
Includes FREE Moon-Cake

The next day, Bob didn't have to start work until the evening. So after some early jumping jacks in the backyard, he bicycled into town to do some errands and see if he could find his best-ever friend.

First he had a quick peek around the modern art gallery. Then he bought two small batteries (to power his rocket), a fancy pair of moon-patterned underpants (on sale for half price), and a newspaper (hot off the press).

The streets were busier than ever. Bob wondered how on earth anyone could hope to find a best-ever friend in a place like **this!**

The Moon

PET SHOW PANDEMONIUM

Asteroid causes chaos by crashing into cages on Pluto.

After his shopping, Bob remembered that Clive and Keith, his cousin Dougal's goldfish, had been looking rather hungry that morning. (Bob was looking after them for a day or two while Dougal was away.)

So Bob headed to the local pet shop, CATS, RATS, 'N' BATS. While he was looking for some "Squishy Delishy Fishy Food" (59 cents), a **strange** notion popped into Bob's head.

Perhaps his best-ever friend could be a **pet!!!**

Bob looked around at all the animals, but he couldn't see anything that looked like a best-ever friend.

To tell you the truth, some of the animals looked a little **odd** to him.

"Oh, well," sighed Bob to himself. "You can't rush these things."

His thoughts were interrupted by the chimes of the town clock. It was four thirty—time for some **tea!**

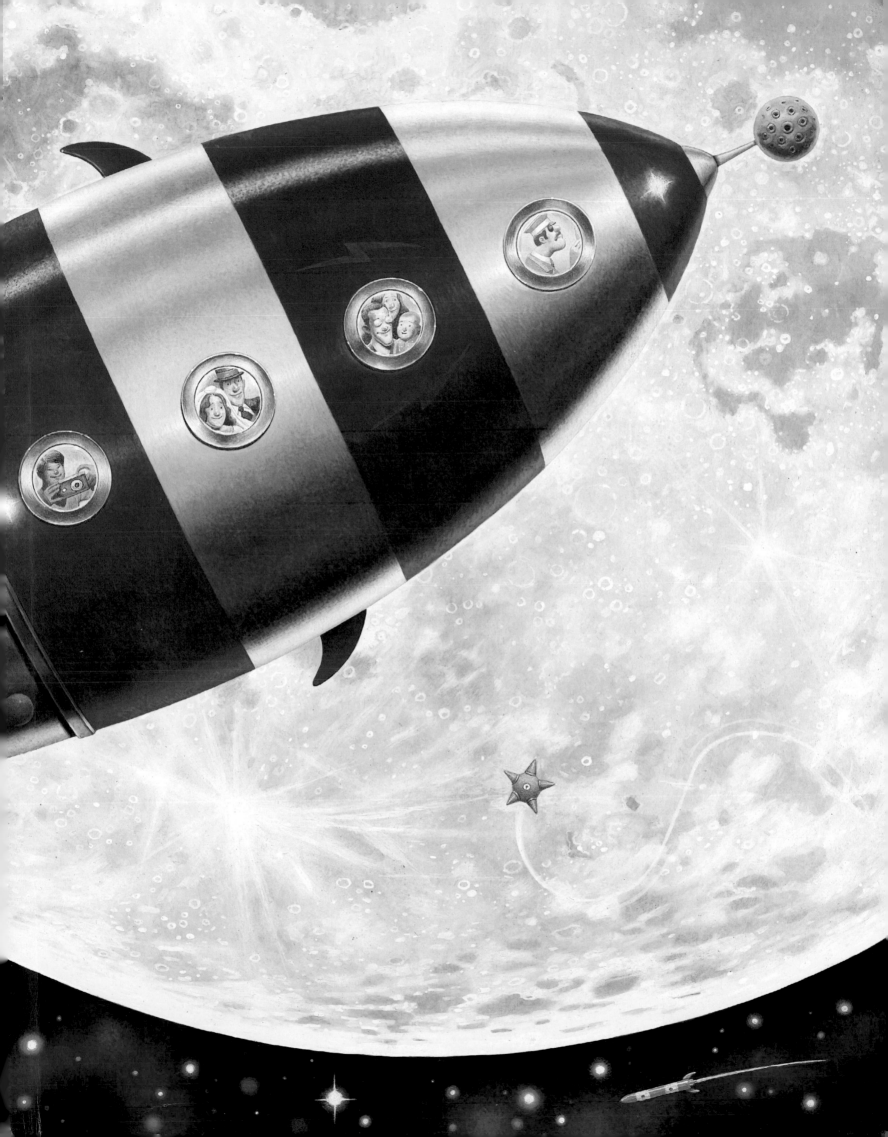

Bob welcomed the tourists with a free Moon Cake and performed his thrilling Moon-themed variety show. Then everyone went home happy.

Everyone, that is, except Bob, who was alone once more. Quietly, he packed away his props and began his weekly crater count.

And that's when it happened!

There, popping out of crater 204, was a little furry tail. What could it be? The closer Bob got to it, the faster the tail wagged and then . . . as if by magic . . . something amazing shot out of the crater.

No one in the **whole** universe would have expected to see what Bob saw at that moment. . . .

It was a dog!!!!

The most smiley, springy dog Bob had **ever** seen.

He had no idea **where** it had come from
or **how** it had gotten there, but he didn't care.
He didn't even care that it looked a little odd.

All Bob knew was that he had finally found his
best-ever friend.

It was as if it had been written in the stars.

Bob named his dog Barry.

And each day, they would go to the Moon and they would **run** and **leap** and **play** with their friends.

Except, of course, on Tuesdays.

On Tuesdays . . .